Living in
Kenya

Ruth Thomson

Photography by David Hampton

SEA-TO-SEA

Mankato Collingwood London

This edition first published in 2007 by
Sea-to-Sea Publications
1980 Lookout Drive
North Mankato
Minnesota 56003

Printed in China

Library of Congress Cataloging-in-Publication Data
Thomson, Ruth, 1949-
    Kenya / by Ruth Thomson.
        p. cm. -- (Living in--)
    Includes index.
    ISBN-13: 978-1-59771-044-2
    1. Kenya--Juvenile literature. 2. Kenya--Social life and customs--Juvenile literature.
    I. Title. II. Series.

DT433.522.T48 2006   2005058177
967.62--dc22

9 8 7 6 5 4 3 2

Published by arrangement with the Watts Publishing Group Ltd, London

Series editor: Ruth Thomson
Series designer: Edward Kinsey
Consultant: Rob Bowden
(EASI-Educational resourcing)
Additional photographs:
Ashley Cameron page 24(l), 29(l)

Contents

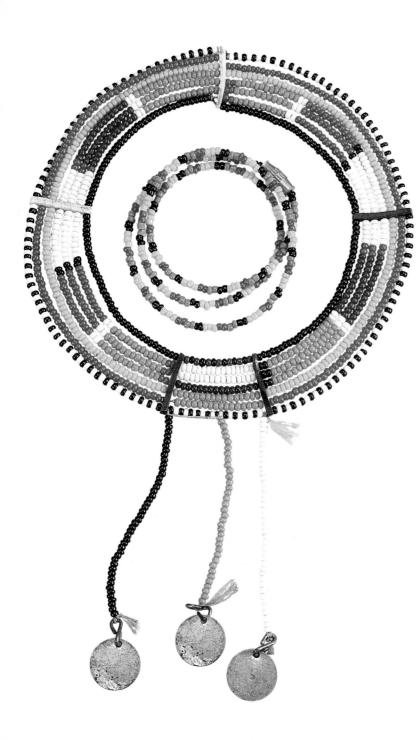

This is Kenya

Kenya is a country in East Africa. It has many different landscapes. The hot north is scrubby desert. In the west are fertile highlands, which drop down to grassy plains. Palms and mangroves grow along the hot, humid coastline to the east of the country.

△**Mount Kenya**
The high peaks of this extinct volcano are covered with snow all year round.

△**The Equator**
The Equator crosses Kenya.

▷**Tribal groups**
There are more than 70 tribal groups in Kenya, each with its own customs. These Samburu graze cattle on the plains around Mount Kenya.

Fact Box
Capital: Nairobi
Population:
30 million
Official languages: Kiswahili and English
Main religion: Christianity
Highest mountain:
Mount Kenya (17,057 ft/5,199 m)
Longest river: Tana
(630 miles/1,014 km)
Biggest cities: Nairobi, Mombasa, Kisumu, Nakuru
Currency: Kenyan shilling (KSh)

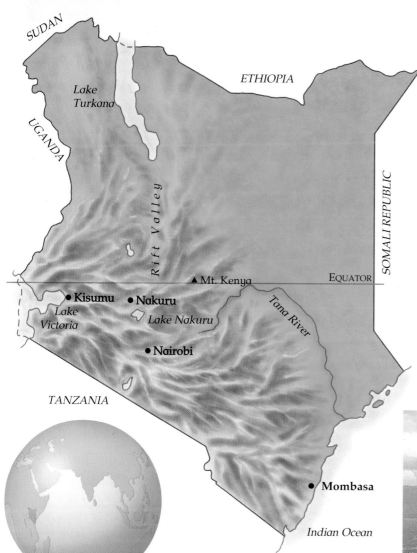

◁ **Picking tea**
Tea plantations cover the wet, fertile slopes of the highlands near Lake Victoria. Tea is one of Kenya's most important cash crops.

▷**The Rift Valley**
This enormous valley runs right through Kenya from north to south. It is dotted with lakes and volcanoes.

Nairobi–the capital

Nairobi started in 1899 as a depot and repair camp for workers building the railroad across the country. It quickly grew into a large town and became the capital. It is now the biggest and most important city in the country.

△ **Walking crowds**
More than two million people live in Nairobi. Those who live in the shantytowns walk into the center to work.

△ **The Uhuru Garden monument**
Kenya was once a British colony. This sculpture of Kenyans raising their national flag celebrates their independence from the British in 1963.

◁ **The city center**
Central Nairobi has some stylish shops, restaurants, and movie theaters, as well as Parliament buildings, museums, and a conference center.

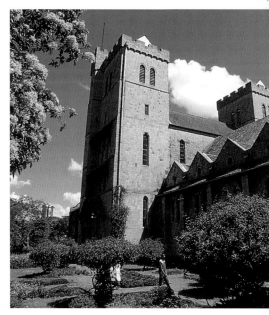

▷All Saints' Cathedral

Most Kenyans are Christian. The country's main cathedral was built by the British.

◁▽A city of contrasts

The city center has many modern offices and hotels. Nearby are the shantytowns where more than half the population of Nairobi live.

▽Modern facilities

There are several new shopping malls and an increasing number of Internet cafes. These are used mainly by the well off.

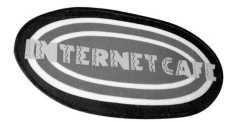

7

Famous sights

The most memorable trip for most visitors to Kenya is a safari to one of its national parks. Mammals, such as wildebeest, giraffes, cheetahs, zebra, antelopes, warthogs, and the "Big Five," roam freely in these protected places.

Some parks have spectacular landscapes, including swamps, gorges, mountains, lakes, geysers, or hot springs.

△**Fort Jesus, Mombasa**
This is one of Kenya's most important historical sights. It was built as a stronghold in 1593, but is now a museum.

▷**Nairobi National Park**
The oldest national park in the country is outside Nairobi. Kenyans, especially school children, visit this as much as tourists.

△**The Big Five**
Tourists who go on safari always hope to spot a lion, buffalo, elephant, leopard, and rhino—the Big Five.

A brochure for one of the national parks

NAIROBI SAFARI WALK

△▽Craft souvenirs
The craft market in Nairobi sells carvings, baskets, and other souvenirs from all over Kenya.

△A paradise for birds
Almost 400 species of birds can be found on Lake Nakuru. More than one million flamingos feed in the shallows.

Living in towns and cities

Fewer than one-third of Kenyans live in towns or cities. However, city populations are growing steadily year by year. The biggest cities are Nairobi and the port of Mombasa. These have great extremes of wealth and poverty.

◁**Public transportation**
Auto rickshaws carry one or two passengers. *Matatus*, privately owned minibuses, can take up to 20 people at a time.

Auto rickshaws

△**Housing**
The better off live in concrete houses or apartments with tiled roofs. The poor live in mud shacks with corrugated iron roofs. These have no running water or electricity.

Matatus

▽**Street child**
Many orphaned children live and work on the streets.

◁▷Street traders

Shoemakers, food stands, and other street sellers have their own regular spots on the sidewalks.

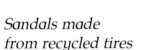

Sandals made from recycled tires

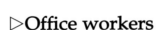

▷Office workers

Well educated people can find office work in banks, businesses, and the government.

People at work

Most city workers work for themselves. Some work in small street workshops, making furniture, shoes, clothes, or metal utensils. Others sell food or goods or offer a service, such as shoe cleaning or haircutting. Large numbers of people have no work at all.

Living in the country

Away from the towns, people live in small settlements scattered across the countryside.

In most places, they live in traditional mud huts with thatched roofs. Elsewhere, people have mud or concrete homes with corrugated iron roofs.

△**The post office**
Villagers go to the nearest post office to collect mail. Letters are put into individual, locked mailboxes.

△**A village street**
Many villages consist of a single, unpaved street. They have a few stores (*dukas*) that stock household basics.

▷**A traditional house**
The pointed, thatched roof keeps a mud house cool and dry.

◁ **Left to dry**
Wet washing is laid over bushes, where it dries quickly. Ironing is done using an iron filled with hot charcoal.

▽**On foot**
Cars are rare in the countryside. Women may walk a long way with their purchases on their heads.

△**Washing clothes**
In places without running water, it is far easier to wash clothes in the river than to bring enough water home for the job.

Working in the country

Four out of five Kenyans work on the land, growing crops either for themselves or to sell. They live mainly in the west or south, where the soil is fertile and there is enough rainfall to water the crops.

Most families own land, called a *shamba*, where they grow their food. They may also keep cows, goats, and sheep for milk or meat.

△**Farming**
Many people use iron hoes to dig the ground. Very few farmers can afford a tractor.

Shamba crops

Sweet potatoes

Yam

Carrots

Cassava

Kidney beans

△**Carving wood**
In places which suffer from drought, it is hard to grow crops. Some people earn money to buy food by making wood-carvings for tourists.

◁**Coffee picking**
Coffee beans grow in the cool, wet highlands. They are picked in December and laid out on long tables to dry in the sun.

Freshly picked coffee beans

▽**Fresh today**
These fresh fruits and vegetables are grown for foreign markets and flown abroad every day.

Mango

Pineapple

Sugar snap peas

Guava

Green beans

Passion fruit

Eggplant

Cash crops

Crops grown to sell abroad provide nearly half of the country's wealth. Kenya produces one-tenth of the world's tea. Other important cash crops are coffee, peas, green beans, sugarcane, and cut flowers, especially roses.

Fuel and water

In most rural areas, houses have no electricity supply, running water, or flush toilets. Women and children have to collect the firewood and water. These are tiring, time-consuming tasks.

△**Collecting firewood**
Children collect fallen branches as fuel for cooking. They look for specific types that do not make too much smoke when they burn.

▷**A charcoal store**
Some people buy charcoal for their cooking stoves (*jiko*).

△**Paraffin lamps**
Villagers use paraffin lamps, candles, or flashlights to light their homes.

Matches

Water supplies

There are two main seasons in Kenya—rainy and dry. However, in the north, water is often scarce and there is a constant threat of drought.

Usually, people collect water from rivers. Sometimes these are polluted and can cause illness.

△Buying water

During the dry season, there is often a water shortage. Some people have to buy water from a water tanker. They store it in plastic containers.

▷Bottled water

Those who can afford it can buy bottled water for drinking. This is safer than river water.

△Collecting water

With a wheelbarrow, children can transport a good quantity of water at a time.

Shopping

Most towns have a weekly market that attracts people from all around. People buy food from women who come to sell the surplus from their *shambas*, as well as from professional traders.

People often buy clothes, shoes, and furniture from the tailors, shoemakers, and carpenters who made them.

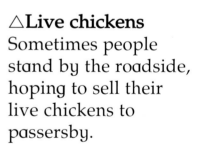

△General store
Villages often have a general store where people can buy drinks, packaged food, fruit, and small household goods.

▷Going to market
Markets are held outdoors. As well as food, traders may sell cooking pots, brushes, earthenware, and second-hand clothes.

△Live chickens
Sometimes people stand by the roadside, hoping to sell their live chickens to passersby.

▷Food measuring

Dry foods are sold by volume, rather than by weight. Amounts are measured by canfuls.

Some packaged goods

Packaging

Very few foods or goods are sold prepackaged. Dry goods are sold from large sacks; meat is cut fresh at the butcher's. Glass and plastic bottles are recycled.

Only factory goods, such as flour, detergent, and margarine, come in packages or cans.

A hardware store

A butcher

On the move

▷**Trains**
The main railroad runs between Nairobi and Mombasa. Trains are are slow and expensive and are no longer an important form of transportation.

Very few Kenyans can afford to buy a car. Most people walk or cycle locally. They travel to the nearest market by *matatu*. People get on and off these minibuses anywhere they like along the route. They use larger buses for longer journeys.

▽▷**Tough bicycles**
Bikes have two cross-bars and covered chains for cycling on bumpy roads. Many villages have repair workshops (*fundi*) for mending the frequent holes in tires.

△**Country roads**
In rural areas, roads are often made of packed earth. These are dusty in the dry season and muddy in the rainy season.

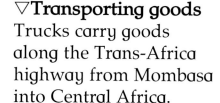

△Ferries
This car ferry travels between Mombasa island and the coast.

▽Transporting goods
Trucks carry goods along the Trans-Africa highway from Mombasa into Central Africa.

△Long-distance buses
Regular buses travel between major towns. They stop at bus stations along the way.

△Donkeys
Donkeys are used in the country to carry crops, firewood, and water.

The roads
The main roads between towns are tarmac, but are often full of potholes. They are not always regularly repaired, so there are often accidents.

Family life

△**Town apartments**
In towns, many families live
in small, crowded apartments.

▽**A compound**
A compound is often built
in a circular shape, like this.

City families live in houses or apartments. In the country, many families live together with their relatives in a compound. This is a collection of several houses, one for each family unit.

These extended families share the separate kitchen and the storehouses for maize and beans. There is also a pen for keeping animals safe at night.
As a family grows in size, new houses may be added to the compound.

△**Cooking**
Women do all the cooking
on an open fire or use
a charcoal stove (*jiko*).

▽**Eating together**
Families share their meal
around a small, low table.
They use enamel dishes.

▷**Boys' jobs**
After school, boys
help fetch water or
look after the farm
animals.

▽**Girls' jobs**
Girls often look after
a smaller brother or
sister. They also
sweep and often do
the dishes.

Time to eat

Millions of Kenyans do not have enough to eat every day. Inexpensive and filling dishes are made from corn, sweet potatoes, and kidney beans. They are often served with a meat sauce. Almost everyone drinks sweet, milky tea (*chai*).

△Breakfast
For breakfast, people usually have a bowl of *uji*. This thin porridge is made from cornflour mixed with sugar and milk.

▷Barbecued meat
People enjoy having barbecued meat (*nyama choma*) at eating places like this one.

△A wealth of fruit
The varied climate means that fruit is available all year round. At different seasons there are bananas, passion fruit, pineapple, oranges, and watermelons.

◁Preserving food

Very few housholds have a fridge, so fish and meat are often preserved to stop them from going rotten.

▷Roast corn

Roadside sellers roast corn on a grill for people to buy as a snack.

▽Using corn

Corn can be dried easily and stored for a long time. It is ground into meal, which is mixed with water and cooked. This sets hard into a dish called *ugali*.

Cornmeal

Ugali

School time

Children can go to primary school for eight years. The government pays for the teachers, but parents often have to raise money for the upkeep and repairs of the school buildings.

Since not every family can afford the school uniform and books, not every child in Kenya goes to school.

△**Going to school**
Country children walk to school. It may take some an hour or more.

▷**Lessons**
Pupils learn practical subjects, including agriculture, carpentry, and domestic science, as well as maths, Kiswahili, English, and science.

△**School facilities**
Most classrooms are in single story blocks. There are separate toilet and washing facilities. There is usually a playing field for games and school assemblies.

26

◁Farming lessons
Rural schools have their own vegetable garden (*shamba*), where pupils work. The produce is sold to raise money for the school.

▷Higher education
Kenya has several universities. The biggest, in Nairobi, has 20,000 students.

Ruler

Pencil

Kiswahili book

Pencil sharpener

English book

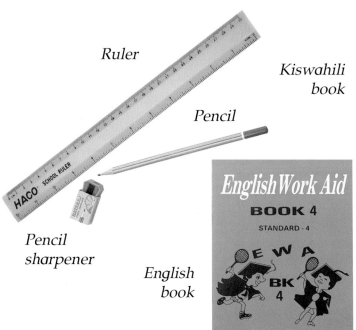

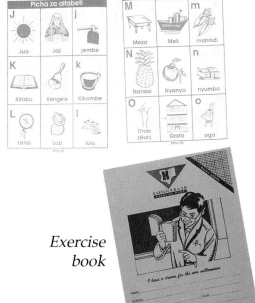

Exercise book

Kiswahili reading books

Having fun

Many Kenyans have very little time for leisure. In the country, there is always work to be done. Few people have money to spare for luxuries. During their free time, many women make crafts, such as baskets, mats, or jewelry, for their own use.

▽**Playing soccer**
Children make soccer balls from plastic bags tightly wound together with string or rubber bands.

△**Soccer shirts for sale**
Many people are fans of English soccer teams. Owning an imported second-hand soccer shirt is much prized.

▽**Time for a snack**
In cities, a favorite treat is a bottle of soda and a bag of potato chips.

◁ Radio
Radio broadcasts are mainly in Kiswahili or English.

▷ Home-made toys
Children recycle wire, scrap tin, wood, string, and fabric to make toys that move.

Wire toy

Time to tune in
Millions of households have battery radios. People listen to the national network, or to local stations that play African and Western pop music. Television is rare, except in the big cities.

Going further

Kenyan fruit and vegetables

Look at the fruit and vegetables in a supermarket to discover which come from Kenya.

Make a list of the foods and their cost per pound. Add some locally produced foods to your list and compare their cost with the Kenyan ones.

Make a safari guide

Find out more about some of the animals you might see in a Kenyan national park.

Make a safari guide, using a piece of paper folded into three. Draw some pictures of the animals or stick down some photographs cut out from color magazines or vacation brochures. Write a short caption about each animal.

Make a wire model

Use some soft wire to make a toy model. You may like to make a bike or a car, as Kenyan children do, or you may prefer to make a spaceship or an airplane. You could also make a person or a building.

Leave the model plain or cover it with strips of scrap fabric.

Websites

www.kenyaweb.com

www.factmonster.com (type in Kenya and click search)

www.worldalmanacforkids.com/explore/nations/kenya.html

Glossary

Cash crop A crop that is grown for sale and not as food for the farmer.

Colony A country that is ruled by people from another country.

Currency The money used by a country.

Drought A long period where there is very little rainfall or none at all.

Equator The imaginary line around the widest part of the Earth, which is an equal distance from the North and South Poles.

Fertile Able to produce a plentiful supply.

Independence The time when a country begins to rule itself, after being ruled by another one.

Geyser A spring that spouts hot water into the air.

Mangroves Tree that grow in muddy swamps on tropical coasts or riverbanks. Their long roots grow above the ground.

Plain An area of flat land.

Plantation Land planted with a single crop, such as tea, coffee, or rubber.

Polluted Dirty and harmful to people, animals, and plants.

Population The total number of people living in a place.

Safari A journey, often in search of wild animals.

Shantytown Unplanned city housing with no power, water supply, sewers, or garbage collection.

Staple The food that people eat every day.

Spring The place where an underground stream comes out to the surface.

Volcano A cone-shaped mountain lying over an underground chamber of molten rock. Sometimes pressure from hot gases causes a volcano to erupt.

Index